A MONSTROUS History

Dear Reader

When I first began to research this book, I knew about some of the more common monsters, such as Count Dracula and Frankenstein's monster. But I quickly realised that, no matter where you are, the world is full of monsters! Whether they exist in reality or only in people's minds, they all seem to serve a common purpose.

WHY DO WE HAVE A FASCINATION FOR TERRIFYING CREATURES THAT WE KNOW CANNOT EXIST?

Every culture around the world has its own monsters, and I hope you enjoy reading about some of them. But, if I were you, I'd check under your desk first! And I'd look over my shoulder, just in case. In fact, what's that behind you **right now**?

John Parsons

Contents

A MONSTROUS History

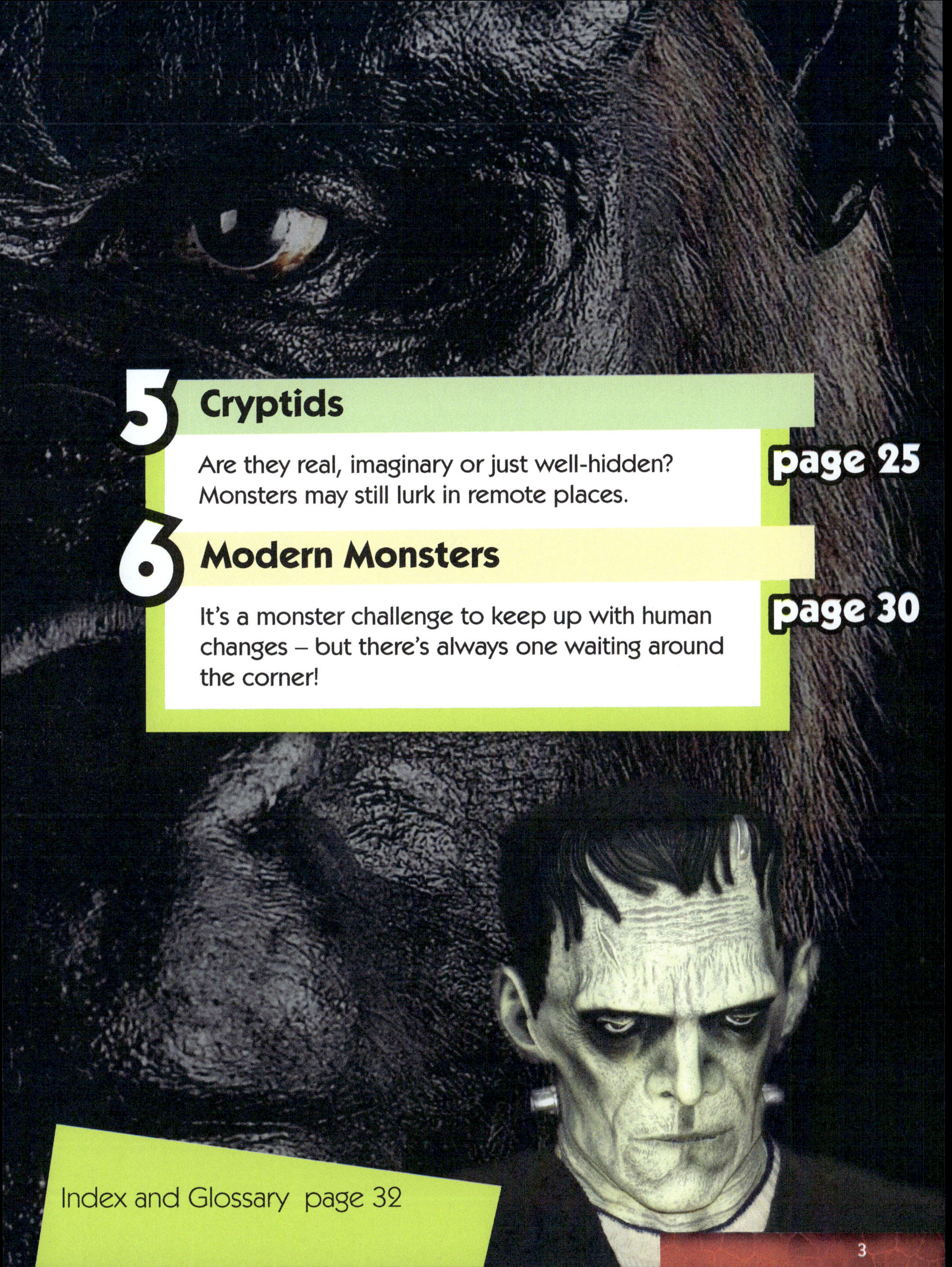

1 Monstro-duction

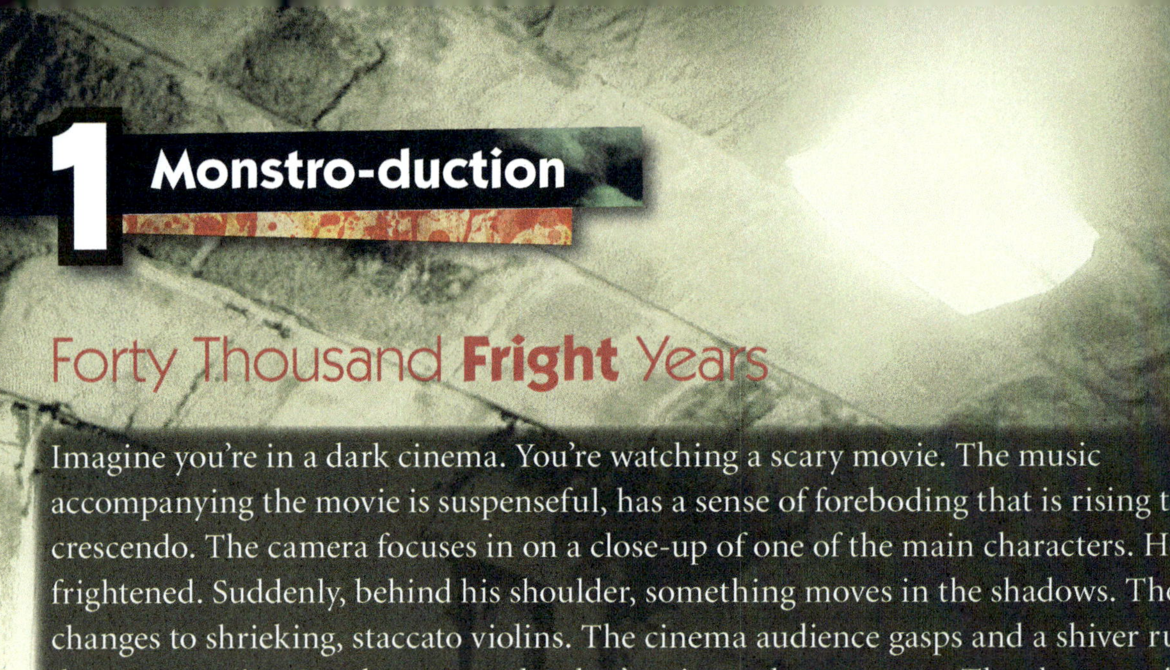

Forty Thousand **Fright** Years

Imagine you're in a dark cinema. You're watching a scary movie. The music accompanying the movie is suspenseful, has a sense of foreboding that is rising to a crescendo. The camera focuses in on a close-up of one of the main characters. He looks frightened. Suddenly, behind his shoulder, something moves in the shadows. The music changes to shrieking, staccato violins. The cinema audience gasps and a shiver runs down your spine. You know exactly what's going to happen next. The character is about to be confronted by his worst nightmare – a terrifying monster lurking in the gloom!

You and the other audience members are participating in a tradition that has probably been around since the earliest humans learned how to communicate. Although modern movies may use digital special effects, grotesque make-up and advanced technology to bring imaginary monsters to life, the themes in scary movies are not that different to those that would have been recounted around the embers of fires lit in caves 40 000 years ago.

What's surprising is that although most monsters are completely imaginary, every culture around the world tells stories about their existence. The concept of monsters is so universal that almost every human being will be exposed to it at some time in their lives – often when they are young.

So what is it about monsters that keeps them in our consciousness, generation after generation? Why do we have a fascination for terrifying creatures that we know cannot exist? Why do we deliberately choose to frighten ourselves by telling tales about horrifying monsters that want to destroy us?

The reason, which has remained unchanged since the Stone Age, may surprise you.

WHAT IS FEAR?

Fear is an emotion caused by a threat, and is a basic survival mechanism. It is our brain's way of recognising danger.

When the brain encounters something it perceives as a threat, a primitive part of the brain called the amygdala instantly releases hormones into the bloodstream. These hormones immediately put the person into a state of heightened alertness. They also increase heart rate, blood flow and breathing rate, which helps muscles prepare for action.

Another part of the brain, the hypothalamus, controls the next stage. The hypothalamus alerts the nerves connected to the muscles to be ready to do one of two things: fight the thing that has caused us fear; or run away from it. This is known as the "fight or flight" response. In a split second, we must decide whether we can overcome the danger or whether we are better to get away from it as fast as possible. All humans and most animals exhibit this behaviour.

a human brain in profile

Once we have either fought or escaped from the cause of our fear, our heart rate, blood flow and breathing returns to normal. The amygdala and certain other parts of the brain, however, record the event as a permanent memory so that we can respond with the benefit of experience next time the threat appears.

2 Why Monsters Exist

A **Survival** Mechanism

Separated by tens of thousands of years, Stone Age monsters and twenty-first century monsters have one thing in common. In fact, all monsters from around the world, regardless of their appearance or behaviour, share a purpose. They are, believe it or not, there to help us.

For all living things, the desire to survive in a difficult and sometimes dangerous world is a fundamental urge. And, for all animals, the desire to protect their young until they are able to fend for themselves is equally powerful. The ability to survive and the drive to ensure your offspring survive helps a species to continue.

Humans share these characteristics. But, unlike other animals, they have a powerful advantage. That advantage is language. Language gives humans the ability to pass on their knowledge about how to survive in threatening or dangerous situations without having to expose themselves to a real threat or danger.

By passing on stories about scary situations, and by frightening a listener with words instead of physical danger, the storyteller may prevent others from actually getting into trouble. Monsters are a "virtual" survival mechanism that has been so effective in keeping us away from dangerous places or threatening situations, that after 40 000 years, they're still around – and still frightening us!

In Stone Age times, monsters such as sabre-tooth tigers (below) would have been very real threats.

WHAT ARE MONSTERS?

In Indigenous Australian culture, the bunyip is a monster that inhabits swamps, creeks and waterways. In the past, stories of bunyips stealing children were common, and children were often warned not to play by rivers, swamps or waterholes at night "in case the bunyip gets you!"

Whether or not bunyips actually exist, the effect of the stories about these monsters was the same. Children, and adults who had heard of bunyips when they were young, avoided waterways at night. At night-time, being in a swampy area or near deep water is inherently dangerous, so fear of the bunyip prevented generations of young Australians from putting themselves at risk of drowning.

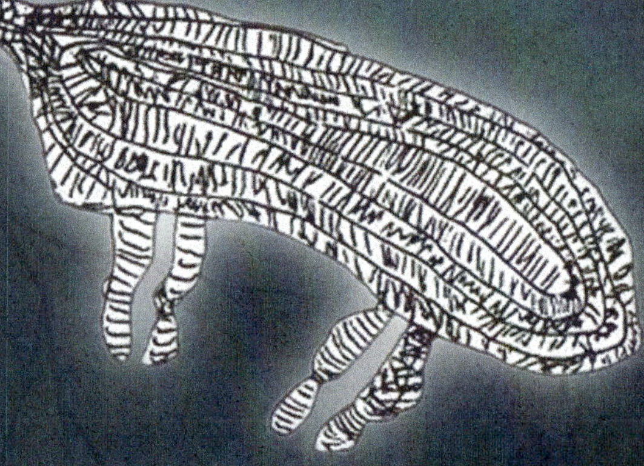

a bunyip, drawn in 1848, by an Indigenous Australian artist known as Kurruk

Since the 19th century, the bunyip has been a popular character in Australian music, pantomime and literature.

Early seafaring cultures, such as the Ancient Greeks, recounted many tales about monsters such as Charybdis and Scylla, who lived near rocky coastlines and in treacherous seas and preyed upon the crews of ships that passed through these areas. Again, whether or not these terrifying sea creatures actually existed, their effect on seafarers who had been frightened by stories about them was very real. The seafarers took extreme caution and kept a close watch on the water when sailing through dangerous areas thought to be inhabited by Charybdis or Scylla. In many cases, fear of being eaten by a sea monster might have actually prevented seafarers from being shipwrecked or lost at sea.

Skurdelgrymm, an evil troll from the Nelson Literacy Directions book The Gryffenstrykke

MONSTER SOCIETY

When early humans from different family groups settled in a location and formed a community, they needed to learn to live together and establish rules about what was acceptable behaviour and what was not. Again, monsters proved to be very helpful in teaching people, especially young people, about why they should obey the rules of the community.

Communities in northern Europe were often small and isolated. Traditional tales from those groups feature badly behaved monsters, such as trolls and ogres. Trolls and ogres invariably cause trouble and strife for any humans nearby. They steal, quarrel, fight and have appalling personal hygiene. They may kidnap, injure or even kill people unfortunate enough to come into contact with them. All of the traits of a troll or an ogre would also be extremely unpleasant in a human, especially one living in a small community where everyone depended upon each other for their wellbeing. Trolls and ogres show what happens when the normal code of behaviour in a culture or society breaks down or is ignored.

WHO ARE YOU?

STRANGER DANGER

Humans have a natural instinct to be cautious around people they do not know. This is a survival mechanism from prehistoric times, when early humans lived in small family groups, often competing with other family groups for resources such as food or water. In early human society, family members could usually be trusted. But strangers were treated with suspicion, as they could well represent a threat to the family group or to their resources.

Monsters help to reinforce the wariness we may have about people who look or behave differently, or who may have come from a place we are not familiar with. Often, monsters might take a human form, with distorted features or an ugly appearance. In prehistoric times, this would mean your level of fear and caution would rise whenever you came across someone who looked different to you; in modern times, we have learned that looking different or coming from a faraway place are not things to worry about, but we still know to exercise caution around strangers we do not know.

Of course you can trust me! I may look like a green-skinned, sharp-toothed, hairy werewolf in human form, but I like to think it's what's on the inside that matters. Don't you?

BE AFRAID, VERY AFRAID!

If you want to survive in a dangerous world, fear is an extremely useful emotion. Early humans who were not afraid to confront deadly predators roaming the grasslands of Africa might have ended up being thought of as brave – or they might have ended up dead.

By contrast, early humans who were quick to fear dangerous situations were more likely to run away, survive and later reproduce. Being afraid of dangerous animals, dangerous behaviours and dangerous environments is a distinct advantage in the survival stakes. Our fascination and fear of monsters are the result of countless generations avoiding and surviving dangerous situations.

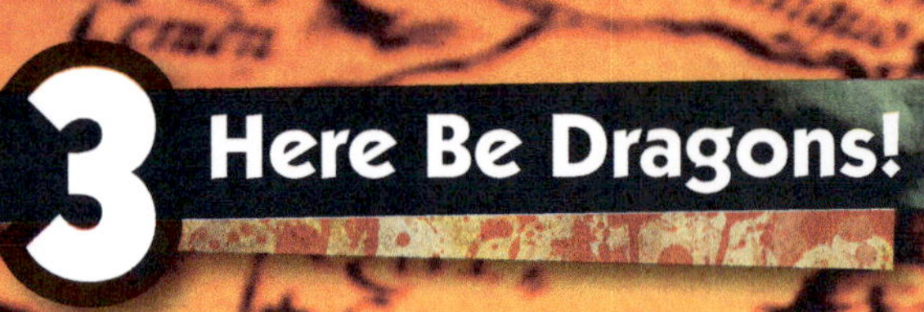

3 Here Be Dragons!

A Frightening World

Before the world had been fully explored, early European mapmakers often filled in unknown parts of maps with fanciful pictures of sea monsters, dragons and other frightening creatures. The Lenox Globe, made in the early 1500s and depicting the known world, included the warning "here be dragons".

This warning served to alert navigators and explorers that these parts of the world were unknown, and could therefore be dangerous. Most navigators, except the most adventurous, avoided these uncharted areas.

The Lenox Globe includes pictures of many of the major monsters from history and where they apparently originated. If you find yourself travelling to one of these places for the first time, you might want to be careful. In the twenty-first century, it's still wise to exercise caution when you're exploring an area that you're unfamiliar with.

the Lenox Globe

THE LENOX GLOBE

The Latin words *hic sunt dracones*, which mean "here be dragons", appear on the Lenox Globe in an area near South-East Asia.

HIC SUNT DRACONES

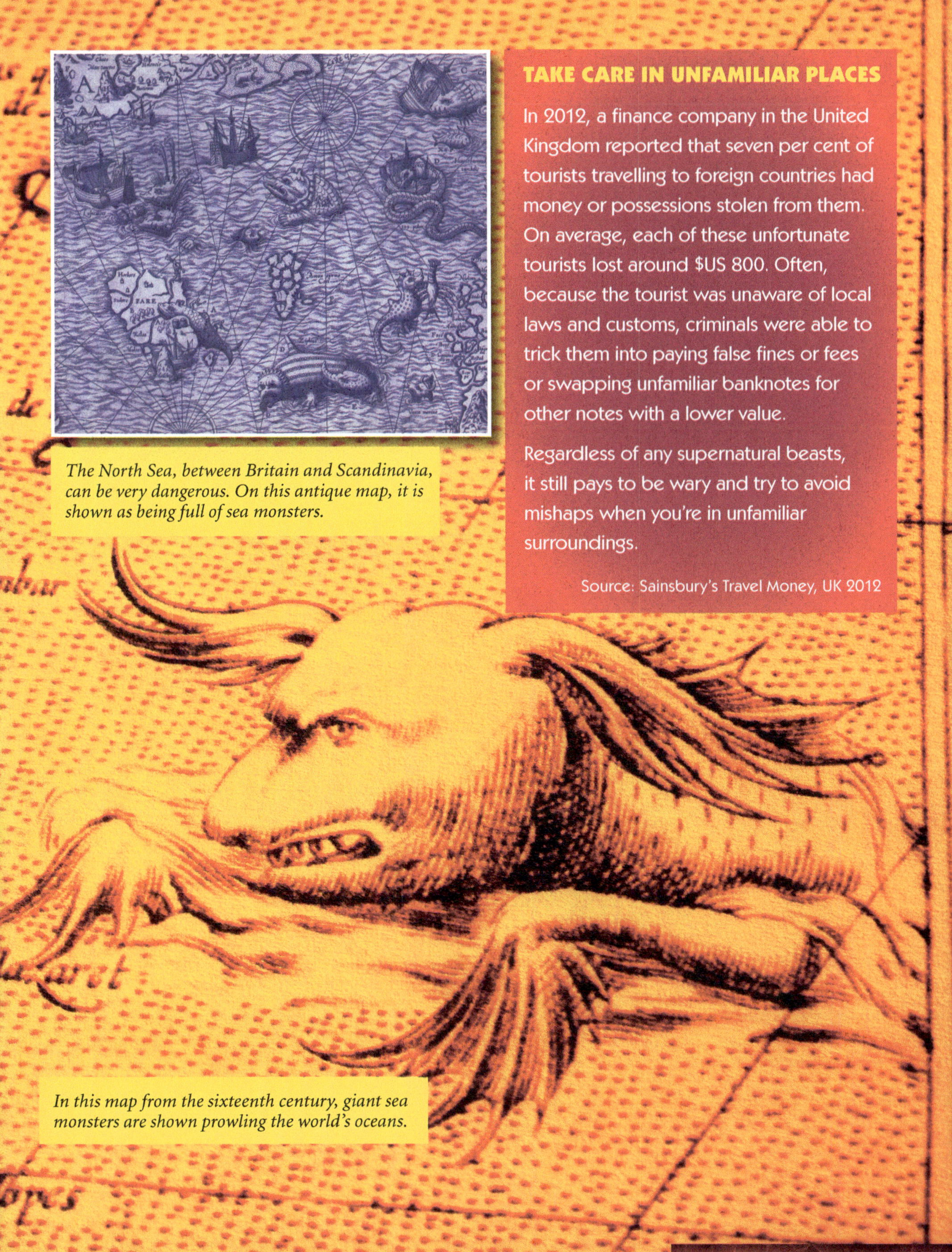

The North Sea, between Britain and Scandinavia, can be very dangerous. On this antique map, it is shown as being full of sea monsters.

TAKE CARE IN UNFAMILIAR PLACES

In 2012, a finance company in the United Kingdom reported that seven per cent of tourists travelling to foreign countries had money or possessions stolen from them. On average, each of these unfortunate tourists lost around $US 800. Often, because the tourist was unaware of local laws and customs, criminals were able to trick them into paying false fines or fees or swapping unfamiliar banknotes for other notes with a lower value.

Regardless of any supernatural beasts, it still pays to be wary and try to avoid mishaps when you're in unfamiliar surroundings.

Source: Sainsbury's Travel Money, UK 2012

In this map from the sixteenth century, giant sea monsters are shown prowling the world's oceans.

Monster Map

Stories from all around the world describe monsters of many different shapes and sizes. Here's just a tiny selection.

GIANTS
Mythical beings of superhuman size, common worldwide
VAMPIRES
A human-like creature that drinks blood
MINOTAUR
A creature with the head of a bull and body of a man
CHINESE DRAGON
A serpentine creature that creates storms and floods
BASAN
A fire-breathing monster chicken
ASIA
JAPAN
HANTU
A demon that takes the form of tigers, forest creatures and humans
BOUDA
A hyena that can change into a human
GARUDA
Part human, part eagle
ROMPO
A creature that feeds only on human corpses
DIRAWONG
A mythical goanna
MOKELE-MBEMBE
A monster that lives in jungle rivers and lakes
YOWIE
A hairy giant
BUNYIP
A water monster with tusks and flippers
AUSTRALIA
DRAGONS
Mythical reptile-like creatures, common worldwide
TANIWHA
A river monster
NEW ZEALAND

4 Monsters of Fiction

A **Fearsome** Read

For hundreds of years, monsters have been a popular subject in literature. Often, it is the theme or situation in which the monster – and the monster's victims – find themselves that makes us feel uneasy. In fact, how the monsters and the other characters feel is often more frightening than the appearance or behaviour of the monster itself.

As with monsters that warn us to avoid dangerous situations, these monsters are also there to help us. Fictional stories about monsters allow us to explore and, to a safe degree, experience many of the things that make us feel uncomfortable without putting ourselves in real danger or discomfort. Monster stories often include themes dealing with isolation, loneliness and extremes of personality. Most readers can identify with the emotions that these things inspire – and therefore the experiences of the monster in the story give us a safe way to understand our own deepest, darkest insecurities.

Five Literary **Monsters** with Feelings

There are many famous monsters in literature that reflect human emotions.

1 DRACULA

In Bram Stoker's book *Dracula*, written in 1897, a vampire comes to England. Count Dracula expresses his desire to escape isolation.

2 THE STRANGE CASE OF DR JEKYLL AND MR HYDE

In this book, written by Robert Louis Stevenson in 1886, Dr Jekyll discovers that a part of his personality, called Mr Hyde, will not obey the rules of well-mannered society.

3

KING KONG

In the screenplay for this movie, first released in 1933, a giant ape longs for companionship, but is rejected in love.

4

THE MUMMY

Jane Loudon's novel of 1827 looks at what happens when an ancient mummy wakes up in the unfamiliar modern world and is unable to adapt to change.

5

FRANKENSTEIN

Mary Shelley's famous novel from 1818 is about a monster that creates havoc because he is lonely and feels rejected.

a portrait of Mary Shelley (1797–1851), first exhibited in 1840 by the artist Richard Rothwell

Creating a **Fictional** Monster

In 1816, an 18-year-old woman named Mary Wollstonecraft Godwin was travelling around Europe with a group of friends, including her future husband, the poet Percy Shelley; Lord Byron, another poet; and Byron's personal doctor, John Polidori. The year before, a volcano in Indonesia called Mount Tambora had erupted with such force that its ash cloud caused worldwide climate anomalies. As a result, the summer of 1816 was wet, cold and gloomy.

The friends were staying in a grand villa in Switzerland. Unable to enjoy themselves outside, Mary and her friends became bored. One evening, Lord Byron suggested that they entertain themselves by having a competition to see who could write the scariest horror story.

Percy Shelley, painted in 1819 by Amelia Curran

Lord Byron, painted by Richard Westall in 1813

During the night, Mary had a strange dream. She dreamt of a scientist who had created a living, breathing replica of a human in his laboratory, and who was horrified by his monstrous creation. When she woke the next morning, she knew she had an idea for her horror story, and she began to write it. She called the scientist who created the monster "Dr Frankenstein". For three weeks, Mary worked on her horror story. At the same time, John Polidori was writing about a different kind of monster – one that lived in the darkness and drank blood. His monster was a vampire.

When Mary's story was finished, her friends read it and thought it was so good that Mary should get it published. Mary returned home to England and worked on her story throughout the rest of 1816 and into early 1817. When she was satisfied that her story was complete, she sent it to two publishers, but both turned the manuscript down. Finally, on her third attempt, a publisher agreed to produce and print her book. In 1818, 500 copies of her book, entitled *Frankenstein; or, the Modern Prometheus*, were published. The publisher did not think that people would buy a horror story written by a woman, so they did not put Mary's name on it. Instead, the book was published anonymously.

INSPIRATION

an illustration from one of the early editions of Frankenstein

Where did Mary find her inspiration for the story of Frankenstein and his monster? Some people have suggested that she and her companions may have visited one of three German castles named Frankenstein on their European travels. In one of these castles, an alchemist called Konrad Dippel was known to have experimented with human corpses. Others say that the title of her book offers a clue. As an educated woman, Mary would have known the Ancient Greek legend of Prometheus, who was ordered by the Greek god Zeus to make the first humans from clay and water.

John Polidori, too, did not at first get credit for his vampire story. It was published without Polidori's permission under the name of Lord Byron. It was only when both Byron and Polidori publically insisted that Polidori was the true author that people believed that Byron, the more famous of the two, had not written it.

Polidori's story of the vampire was popular, but it could not compete with the notoriety of Mary's *Frankenstein*. In 1822, the publisher finally decided to reveal the true identity of *Frankenstein*'s author. When people discovered the book had been written by a woman, they were astounded because it was widely believed at the time that such writing was not natural to women.

It's amazing to think that from the boredom of a rainy night, two of the most enduring monsters of popular fiction – Frankenstein's monster and vampires – were created. Though both authors published other works, they are remembered most for the spine-chilling monsters they created. These monsters have inspired films, music, fashion and many other novels, and they continue to scare us today, just as they scared people nearly two hundred years ago.

"A VILE INSECT"

FRANKENSTEIN'S MONSTER

Many people think that Frankenstein is the name of the monster in Mary Shelley's book. But Frankenstein is actually the name of the monster's creator, not the monster itself. In fact, the monster doesn't have a name. In the book, it is known as the "monster", "creature", "demon", "devil", "wretch", "vile insect", "abhorred monster", "fiend" and "wretched devil". Not giving the monster a name makes it even more threatening and frightening.

5 Cryptids

Real or Imaginary?

Cryptids are animals that many people claim exist, but for which there is no scientific evidence. Often, these animals take the form of monsters. Some cryptids, such as the Loch Ness monster, are harmless and non-threatening. Others, such as the chupacabra, are reputed to be bloodthirsty and dangerous. The study of animals that may or may not exist is called cryptozoology.

an artist's impression of the Loch Ness monster

CRYPTOZOOLOGY

The term "cryptozoology" was first used in 1955 by Belgian zoologist Bernard Heuvalmans. It combines the Greek word *kryptos*, which means "hidden", with "zoology", which is the study of animals. Cryptozoology is therefore the study of hidden animals.

Most mainstream scientists dismiss cryptozoology as the result of traditional tales and legends that have no basis in fact. But cryptozoologists point out that before the nineteenth century, real animals, such as the giant squid and the mountain gorillas of central Africa, were also thought to be just the result of fanciful imaginations. Perhaps the fact that scientific evidence for these monstrous creatures continues to elude us makes them even more fascinating!

THE LOCH NESS MONSTER

Stories of a strange water-beast inhabiting the Scottish lake called Loch Ness first began around the fifth century. To this day, people remain fascinated with the possibility of a monster living in the lake.

Many people believe that the Loch Ness monster might be some kind of ancient reptile, related to prehistoric plesiosaurs. Others dismiss it as a hoax or wishful thinking. Photography, sonar, video and submarines have all been used to try and verify the existence of this cryptid, but there has been no conclusive proof that there is an actual Loch Ness monster.

In the early 1930s, photographs of what was claimed to be the Loch Ness monster caused great excitement when they were published in newspapers. However, none of those photographs (or any taken since) have been proven to be authentic. Many researchers conclude that, like the one above, they are fakes.

THE MOKELE-MBEMBE

Large lake-dwelling creatures that resemble plesiosaurs feature in many traditional tales from around the world. In central Africa, a creature known as the mokele-mbembe is reputed to inhabit deep pools and stretches of jungle river, occasionally attacking animals and humans. It is described as having an elephant-like body and a long neck, just like the Loch Ness monster.

LOCH NESS

Loch Ness is a large freshwater lake in the Scottish Highlands. It has a depth of 226 metres at its deepest point, and is approximately 36 kilometres long. Because of the peaty areas surrounding it, the waters of Loch Ness can often appear muddy and have poor visibility, which has hampered expeditions that have tried to search underwater for any large creature living there.

SASQUATCH

The sasquatch, sometimes known as "Big Foot", is a large, ape-like creature reputed to live in the remote areas of northwest United States and western Canada. Many indigenous North American tribes have traditional stories about giant wild creatures that appear to be half-human, half-animal. In the 1950s, there were several reported discoveries of large, unusual footprints in the wilderness areas of northern California and, since then, many attempts have been made to capture a sasquatch on film or video. Many photographs have turned out to be hoaxes, but reports of sasquatch sightings continue, especially along the North American Pacific coastline.

a blurry photo that purports to show a North American sasquatch

THE ABOMINABLE SNOWMAN

Many cultures have traditional tales about large hairy creatures resembling humans. In the remote mountainous regions of the Himalayas, which extend across southern Asia, these creatures are known as yeti, or "abominable snowmen". Although no pictures exist of the yeti, many locals and foreign mountaineers have reported sightings or large footprints in the snow.

THE CHUPACABRA

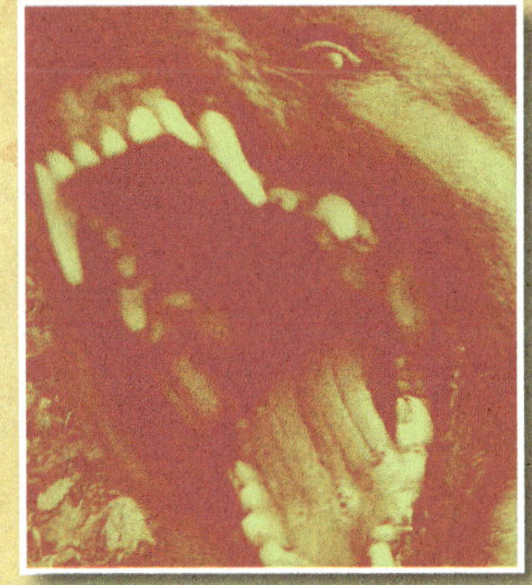

Unlike many cryptids, which have featured in traditional tales for centuries, the chupacabra is a modern phenomenon.

In 1995, in the US territory of Puerto Rico, hundreds of sheep, goats and other farm animals were reportedly killed by a mysterious animal that was said to resemble a small bear with a row of reptilian spines from head to tail, and was referred to as a chupacabra.

Most scientists consider sightings of the chupacabra to be those of mistakenly identified wild dogs. On rare occasions where farmers have managed to shoot what they thought was a chupacabra, it has turned out to be a coyote or a cross-bred coyote–wild dog.

THE MONGOLIAN DEATH WORM

the remote Gobi desert in Mongolia

The frighteningly named Mongolian Death Worm is a massive red worm that is supposed to live beneath the sands of the Gobi desert in central Mongolia. Stories of this cryptid are common among nomads who live in the desert, and it has been blamed for several deaths. The death worm, say the nomads, surprises its victims by emerging from the sand and spitting deadly venom in their direction. Expeditions in search of the Mongolian Death Worm were mounted in the 1990s, but no evidence was found to verify its existence.

6 Modern Monsters

New Unknowns

Most monsters have been part of the human experience for hundreds or even thousands of years. Whether you believe they really exist or consider them to be a way of warning us to keep away from danger, monsters are a part of human consciousness that many people embrace. Even today, we invent monsters to suit our twenty-first century world. Today's most popular monsters are aliens from outer space, and hundreds of movies and books have been created that continue to frighten us with tales of strange, unknown and threatening life forms from other planets.

It's interesting to reflect that the purpose of these alien monsters remains the same as those that the earliest humans frightened themselves with around camp fires 40 000 years ago.

Humans still use the concept of monsters to keep themselves safe, whether that means safe from known danger, society's disapproval, or the risk of the unknown. In generations past, the "unknown" may have been the wilderness, other cultures or the dark of night. Today, it is space, extreme science and unfamiliar technology. Our horizons have expanded – but, tens of thousands of years after the first humans walked on Earth, our natural instinct for caution is still present.

Index

Glossary

anomalies Things that differ from what is considered normal or usual

anonymously Without the author or origin being known

crescendo A gradual increase in force or loudness

foreboding A feeling or impression of something about to happen, especially something bad

inherently Having a permanent and natural attribute

predators Creatures that live by harming other creatures, for food or other gain

navigators People who conduct explorations by sea

phenomenon A thing, fact or occurrence, often remarkable or unusual in some way

replica A copy or reproduction of something

sonar A method of mapping or exploration underwater using sound